PUFFIN BOOKS

King Max the Last

Dick King-Smith served in the Grenadier Guards during the Second World War, and afterwards spent twenty years as a farmer in Gloucestershire, the county of his birth. Many of his stories are inspired by his farming experiences. Later he taught at a village primary school. His first book, *The Fox Busters*, was published in 1978. Since then he has written a great number of children's books, including *The Sheep-Pig* (winner of the *Guardian* Award and filmed as *Babe*), *Harry's Mad*, *Noah's Brother*, *The Hodgeheg*, *Martin's Mice*, *Ace*, *The Cuckoo Child* and *Harriet's Hare* (winner of the Children's Book Award in 1995). At the British Book Awards in 1992 he was voted Children's Author of the Year. He has three children, twelve grandchildren and two great-grandchildren, and lives in a seventeenth-century cottage a short crow's-flight from the house where he was born.

Some other books by Dick King-Smith

ANIMAL STORIES
BLESSU
CLEVER DUCK
DUMPLING
GEORGE SPEAKS
THE GHOST AT CODLIN CASTLE
AND OTHER STORIES
THE HODGEHEG
THE INVISIBLE DOG
MORE ANIMAL STORIES
MR POTTER'S PET
A NARROW SQUEAK AND
OTHER ANIMAL STORIES
PHILIBERT THE FIRST AND OTHER STORIES
SMASHER
THE SWOOSE

Young Puffin Read It Yourself books

HOGSEL AND GRUNTEL
HUGE RED RIDING HOOD
THE JENIUS
ROBIN HOOD AND HIS MISERABLE MEN
THINDERELLA
TRIFFIC: A RARE PIG'S TALE

DICK KING-SMITH

A Hodgeheg Story

King Max the Last

Illustrated by Linda Birch

PUFFIN BOOKS

PUFFIN BOOKS

Published by the Penguin Group
Penguin Books Ltd, 27 Wrights Lane, London W8 5TZ, England
Penguin Putnam Inc., 375 Hudson Street, New York,
New York 10014, USA
Penguin Books Australia Ltd, Ringwood, Victoria, Australia
Penguin Books Canada Ltd, 10 Alcorn Avenue, Toronto,
Ontario, Canada M4V 3B2
Penguin Books (NZ) Ltd, Private Bag 102902, NSMC,
Auckland, New Zealand

On the worldwide web at: www.penguin.com

Penguin Books Ltd, Registered Offices: Harmondsworth,
Middlesex, England

First published by Hamish Hamilton 1995
Published in Puffin Books 1996
11

Set in Baskerville

Made and printed in England by Clays Ltd, St Ives plc

British Library Cataloguing in Publication Data
A CIP catalogue record for this book is available from
the British Library

ISBN 0–140–37257–1

Chapter 1

"THERE'S ONE!" said the man with the torch. "Get him!"

The man with the net popped it neatly over the hurrying hedgehog. Though neither of the men could know this, they had in fact caught a most unusual hedgehog, none other than Victor Maximilian St George, known to his family as Max.

Some time ago, while trying to find a way for hedgehogs to cross busy roads in safety, Max had been hit by a passing cyclist and this had caused him to muddle his words. So that, as he told his family, "Something bot me on the hittom, and then I headed my bang. My ache bads headly." For some while after that, he considered himself to be a hodgeheg.

A second accident had restored Max's mind to normal, and indeed he had succeeded in his task, and had thus become something of a hero to hedgehogkind.

But now, on this particular evening, he felt anything but heroic as the net dropped over him. He rolled himself into a tight ball, his heart hammering in fright.

"Stick him in this sack," said the man with the torch.

"OK," said the man with the net. "He's not all that old, by the size of him. He'll do nicely."

Max's family lived in the garden of Number 5A in a row of suburban houses, and when dawn broke, they were worried.

"Ma! Pa! Our Max hasn't come home!" squeaked his three sisters, Peony, Pansy and Petunia.

"Don't fret," said Ma Hedgehog. But she did.

"He'll turn up in a minute," said

Pa. But he didn't.

From Number 5B next door, the neighbour poked his head through the hedge. He was an elderly bachelor hedgehog, who was fond of Ma and Pa's children. They called him Uncle B.

"What's up?" said Uncle B. "Something wrong?"

"Max hasn't come home," said Pa.

"Went across to the Park last evening, hunting. Hasn't returned."

"He probably decided to stay there and have a good day's sleep," said Uncle B. in a comforting voice.

"But suppose . . . ?" said Ma, and then she stopped.

"No, no," said Uncle B. "Don't even think of it. If there's one hedgehog in the world that knows all about road safety, it's your young Max."

Young Max was, at that very moment, sitting in a wire cage in a laboratory at the University. The scientists who had captured him – their names were Dandy-Green and Duck – were making a study of hedgehog behaviour, and they needed to learn as much as possible of the creatures' nightlife.

5

"Now then," said Dr Dandy-Green, "we'll fit him with a radio collar."

"And then we can follow his movements," said Professor Duck.

But that was easier said than done, they found.

To begin with, when they opened the cage door and (with gloves on) lifted Max out, he rolled himself up. And even if he hadn't, they realized, fitting a collar to a hedgehog is an impossible task. For a start, a hedgehog has no neck to speak of, and anyway there's no method of getting any sort of collar to stay on, on top of all those prickles.

They put Max back in the cage.

"It's hopeless," said Professor Duck. "We might just as well let him go."

"Not yet," said Dr Dandy-Green. "Maybe we'll think of something."

So they sat and thought.

Max sat and thought too. Where was he? What was this place? Who were these men? Why had they caught him? What was to become of him? How he longed to be back at Number 5A with Ma and Pa and Peony and Pansy and Petunia and good old Uncle B. next door.

Thinking of Uncle B. reminded him that the men had put a saucer of Munchimeat dog-food (the old hedgehog's favourite) in the cage. No point in starving to death, said Max to himself, and he began to tuck in.

"He's eating," said the doctor.

"Yes," said the professor. "He's a nice healthy young specimen. Pity we can't make use of him."

"You haven't thought of any way of attaching a transmitter to him?"

7

"No. Afraid not. I'm absolutely stuck."

"Stuck?" said Dr Dandy-Green. "Stuck! That's it!"

"What's what?" asked Professor Duck.

"That's the way to fix the transmitter. Stick it to him!"

"With superglue?"

"Yes! Stick it to the spines on the back of his head. Then we can locate him in the dark."

"Brilliant!" said the professor. "And I'll tell you what – we could fit him with a little flashing light. Run it off the same batteries. Then we can spot him in the dark."

"Great idea!" said the doctor.

They stood up and stared into Max's cage.

Max stared back.

"Wonder what he's thinking?" said Dr Dandy-Green.

"I expect," said Professor Duck, "that he's wishing he was back at home with his family."

I wish I was back at home with my family, thought Max.

"He will be," said the doctor.

"Just as soon as we've fixed him up," said the professor. "He's going to be a most unusual hedgehog, he is."

Chapter 2

WHEN A COUPLE of days had gone by
with no sight of Max, the family at
Number 5A had almost given up hope
of ever seeing him again. Ma was
convinced he had been run over, even
though Pa and Uncle B. had patrolled
all the local roads and reported no
squashings. Peony, Pansy and Petunia,
who were romantic girls, thought Max
had fallen in love and was busy
courting. They whispered and giggled
a lot together.

Pa decided that Max had simply left
home to seek his fortune in the wide
world.

"Didn't even bother to say goodbye," he grumbled.

Uncle B. said nothing, but he was sad, for he was especially fond of Max. He searched the Park from end to end – in the Ornamental Gardens, around the Bandstand, and beside the Lily-Pond – and met a number of foraging hedgehogs but found no sign of his young friend.

Meanwhile the scientists' plans were going forward. They had prepared a very small battery-powered radio transmitter, and had mounted on top of it a little electric lamp that revolved, like the beam of a lighthouse, throwing out a blue light.

Now all they had to do was to fix it to Max.

In fact this turned out to be easy,

especially as by now Max had become used to them and no longer rolled up when handled.

They smeared superglue on the base of the transmitter and over the spines on the back of Max's neck, and managed, while Max was busy with his Munchimeat, to press the two surfaces together for long enough for the glue to set hard.

"How about that?" said Dr Dandy-Green.

"Just the job," said Professor Duck. "It looks as though he is wearing a crown."

"Other hedgehogs should be very impressed, especially when his little light is flashing," said Dr Dandy-Green. "What with that and the transmitter, we'll be able to follow him wherever he goes."

As for Max, he hardly noticed the contrivance, for it weighed very little, and, placed as it was, there was no way that he could actually see it. All he thought about was freedom. Granted, he was well fed, but he was also fed up.

He would have been very happy if he could have understood what was said next.

"When shall we release him?" said Dr Dandy-Green.

"Tomorrow evening?" said Professor Duck. "When we've tested the equipment?"

"OK. Where shall we release him?"

"In that park where we caught him, I should think. That's probably his home territory."

"He ought to have a name or a

number or something," said the doctor.

"Yes," said the professor. "When we're writing up notes on his movements, we don't want to have to write 'the hedgehog did this or that' every time."

They looked at Victor Maximilian St George, wearing (though he did not know it) his crown.

"We need something short," said Dr Dandy-Green.

"How about 'E.E.'?" said Professor Duck.

"E.E.?"

"Yes. The initials of his Latin name, Erinaceus Europaeus."

"E.E. it is!"

So the following day they tested the equipment, allowing Max to trot around the laboratory floor and up and

down the corridors, while they took
turns in holding the receiver and
following him about. All worked
perfectly. The transmitter transmitted,
the receiver received, and the flashing
light flashed.

This last thing puzzled Max since he
could not see where the intermittent
blue light was coming from, but he
soon grew used to it. He was
disappointed to be put back into his

cage, but then, that evening, he left it for good.

What happened next is best described by the notes which Professor Duck and Dr Dandy-Green wrote up the following day.

10.30 pm. Took E.E. to Park, released beside Bandstand. E.E. raised snout, scented air, set off NNW across Park towards nearest road (B 7216), travelling fast. This route involved skirting Lily-Pond and cutting through Ornamental Gardens where it was not easy to observe light in dense shrubbery, flower-beds, etc, and radio contact was needed. In open ground E.E.'s light easily visible. Nervous moments on E.E.'s arrival at road since evening traffic still moderately busy. Astonished to observe E.E. waiting patiently at kerbside until road was quite clear. E.E. then looked left, looked right, looked left again, and calmly crossed, revolving light flashing. Fortunately, this phenomenon was observed by Prof D. and Dr D-G. only. E.E. then went under a gate (Number 5A) and into a suburban garden. Looking over garden wall, Prof D. and Dr D-G. saw several hedgehogs which all fled at E.E.'s approach. Continued observation however revealed that these animals (2 adults and 3 juveniles) returned cautiously after a while and were then joined by another adult from the garden of Number 5B. Much squeaking, grunting, and cough-like snorts ensued. Waited some time but E.E. seemed unwilling to move further, so discontinued observation at 11.43 pm.

The family at Number 5A had been quietly snail-hunting in the rockery

when suddenly under the gate had
come the strangest apparition. It
looked like Max, it smelled like Max,
but what was that strange object on its
head, and what was that ghastly blue
light that flickered round and round
and lit them up in turn? For an instant
they froze in terror, and then Ma
squealed, "It's his ghost! It's our
Max's ghost, come to haunt us!" and
they all scuttled for cover.

Max stood in the middle of the lawn and called, "Ma! Pa! Girls! It's only me. I'm home."

Pa was first out of the flower-bed. He approached Max cautiously, blinking each time the flashes passed over him.

"Is it really you, son?" he said.

"Yes, Pa."

"What's that thing on your head?"

"I can't see it, Pa," Max said.

Peony, Pansy and Petunia came forward.

"Oo!" they squeaked. "Look at Max's hat! Isn't it pretty! Can we have hats like that, Ma?"

Ma shuffled nervously nearer.

"Oh Max!" she said. "Whatever's happened to you?"

Max was about to tell them all about being captured by the two men and put in a cage, but just then Uncle B. came pushing through the hedge. He saw Max and stopped dead in his tracks.

"Oh no!" he said softly. "It cannot be!"

"It is!" the others cried. "It's our Max!"

"But cannot you see what he is wearing?" said Uncle B. "Have you never heard of the legend of the King?"

"What king?" they said.

"Why!" cried Uncle B. "The King of the Hedgehogs! See his crown of light! Your boy Max has been chosen to rule over hedgehogkind!"

Have I? thought Max. King of the Hedgehogs, eh? Sounds a bit of all right, that does.

He lowered his head so that the blue

light shone more brightly upon them all.

"Bless you, my people," he said.

Chapter 3

EVERYONE REACTED IN a particular way
to this new and so different Max.

Old Uncle B. was overcome with
joy. As a very young lad he had first
heard from his mother the story of the
Hedgehog King who would one day
appear. But he had never dreamed
that he should witness this appearance!
And that it should be his young
friend Max, of all hedgehogs! He
remembered that First Crossing, when,
before the astonished eyes of the
lollipop lady, they had all followed
Max over the busy road in perfect
safety.

I should have known, thought Uncle B., that he was destined for greatness.

Ma was awestruck.

"I am the mother of a king," she kept repeating to herself in a dazed fashion.

Pa was puzzled. Whoever heard of a hedgehog wearing a crown, a crown, what's more, that flashed blue light? Yet here was his son, doing just that. He's big-headed enough already, thought Pa. Who knows what he'll be like now he's got all that stuff on his head too.

As for Peony, Pansy and Petunia, they were thrilled to bits. If Max was King, they knew what they must be, and they frisked about the garden, squeaking, "I'm Princess Peony!", "I'm Princess Pansy!" and "I'm Princess Petunia!"

So excited were they that they did not see a shadowy shape approaching.

At the sight of the three young hedgehogs gambolling on the lawn, the fox stood stockstill, his muzzle pointing towards them, his brush straight out behind him, one forepaw raised. He much liked the taste of hedgehog, especially tender young hedgehog.

He was a town fox born and bred,
expert at tipping the lids off dustbins
and undoing the doors of rabbit
hutches, and he had devised a way of
dealing with hedgehogs. Tightly curled
into a ball, they were safe from most
foxes, but this one had his own method
(and a rather disgusting method it
was) of making a hedgehog unroll,
when a quick bite to the stomach
would put an end to it.

He moved forward, and now, seeing
him and smelling him, Peony, Pansy
and Petunia hastily rolled up.

Standing above the nearest one (it
was Pansy), the fox prepared to cock
his leg, just like a dog on a lamp-post,
when suddenly Max appeared around
the corner of Number 5A.

To his horror he saw a fox standing
over one of his sisters.

Then, to his amazement, he saw the fox whisk away and leap the garden wall and disappear, its nerves shattered by the sight of a hedgehog wearing a crown of flashing light.

He was scared of me, thought Max. He was frightened of me, that fox was, that's why he ran away. And why was he frightened?

Because of my crown of light!

Because he too thought that I was the King of the Hedgehogs! Suppose I am?

"Come on now, you girls," he said. "You can uncurl now. The fox has gone. I saw him off."

"Oh Max!" cried Peony, Pansy and Petunia. "Your Majesty! You're wonderful!"

Yes, said Max to himself, I suppose I am. Just fancy! King Max the First, the head of the Royal Family. Hang on though, you can't have a family without a wife. What I need is a Queen!

"Look, girls," he said to his sisters, "I expect you've got lots of friends around the place, up and down the road, and over in the Park, haven't you?"

They giggled.

"Boyfriends, d'you mean?" they said.

"No, no," said Max. "I mean girls, of about your own age."

Peony, Pansy and Petunia looked at one another and tittered.

"Yes," they said. "Lots."

"Pretty, are they?" asked Max in an offhand way.

"Some are," they said.

To humans of course, even to skilled observers like Professor Duck and Dr Dandy-Green, all hedgehogs look alike. Males are a little larger than females, but one animal looks much like another.

Hedgehogs themselves however can see all sorts of differences between individuals. The look in the eye, the pitch of the voice, the walk – all these can make one hedgehog more attractive than another.

Max's sisters had always considered him good-looking, but now, with his crown of light, they thought him the handsomest hedgehog boar that ever was, whose bride must be the most beautiful sow.

"Well, you might spread the word around," said Max. "It's time I got fixed up."

"You mean . . . ?" said Peony, and then she stopped.

"You mean you want . . . ?" said Pansy, and then she stopped.

"You mean," said Petunia, "you want to get married?"

"Possibly," said Max in a bored sort of voice. "At any rate, if any of your friends are interested, tell them to turn up tomorrow night."

"Where?" asked Peony.

"Well, not here," said Max. "There's no need for Ma and Pa to know anything about it, nor Uncle B. They'd only start lecturing me about the importance of making the right choice of wife and all that."

"Where then?" asked Pansy.

"In the Park," said Max.

"Where in the Park?" asked Petunia.

Max thought. "At the Bandstand," he said. "Plenty of room in there, and sheltered if it rains. You'd better go now and then you can be back by dawn. And mind how you cross the road."

"OK, Your Majesty," they said, and they trotted off, giggling like mad.

The following night Professor Duck and Dr Dandy-Green came out with their receiver to record the movements of E.E.

They began at Number 5A, but there was no radio contact nor sign of E.E.'s light, so they crossed to the Park and began a thorough search. They had no luck in the open spaces, nor by the Lily-Pond, nor in the Ornamental Gardens, but as they neared the Bandstand, the receiver began to pick up signals.

Moving very quietly and cautiously, the professor and the doctor approached, to be rewarded by the sight of that flashing blue light. What they then saw is once again best described by their notes.

10.30 pm. Commenced search (Prof D. operating receiver) at Number 5A, where E.E. was last sighted. No contact, so removed to Park.

11.43 pm. Located E.E. at Bandstand. Clear signals, and light working well. At first could only see E.E. motionless in exact centre of circular interior of Bandstand. However light flashes revealed a number of other hedgehogs present.

12.02 am. Fortunately moon rose and revealed scene. At one side of circle three juveniles (females?) side by side (remained

33

so throughout proceedings), squeaking a good deal (excitement?). At other side Dr D-G. counted 15 hedgehogs waiting in a queue *(note: this point is emphasized: no previous recorded instance of such behaviour). At some signal (from E.E.?) animal at head of queue proceeded into centre of circle and walked up and down several times in front of E.E. (as though seeking approval: Dr D-G. reminded of fashion show – models on catwalk) before exiting from Bandstand and disappearing. Each hedgehog in queue performed similarly in turn, parading before E.E., lit by blue flashes from E.E.'s light. E.E. watched each carefully. No means of determining the sex of these animals but none showed aggression towards E.E. as young males might have, and general behaviour suggests they were all females. Could E.E. possibly have been making a*

34

choice of mate? No sign of his having done so. When last had left, the three juvenile spectators came forward to E.E. (Both Prof D. and Dr D-G. suspect these are the three juveniles observed in the garden of Number 5A the previous night, probably E.E.'s siblings.) Again, much squeaking, grunting and snorting occurred. Observation discontinued 12.55 am.

"Well?" cried Peony, Pansy and Petunia excitedly. "What did you think, Max? See anyone you fancied?"

"A few of them weren't too bad," said Max loftily. "But there wasn't one fit for a king."

Chapter 4

IN THE NEXT door garden Pa and Uncle
B. were chatting. Number 5A's people
only ever put out bread-and-milk for
their hedgehogs, whereas the people in
Number 5B were more sensible and
offered Munchimeat. Uncle B. could
never manage all they gave him, and
there was an open invitation for Pa to
come over and help him out whenever
he felt like it, which was often.

Pa swallowed a final mouthful.

"Look here, B.," he said. "Tell me
straight, hog to hog. Do you really
believe in this Hedgehog King
business?"

"Absolutely, my dear fellow," said Uncle B. "I'm only surprised that your parents never told you of the legend."

"They died when I was very young," said Pa. "Heavy lorry. On the main road out of town. Flattened the pair of them."

"In their death they were not divided," said Uncle B. gravely.

"Dead right," said Pa.

"How proud they would have been of their grandson Max," said Uncle B. "Or King Max, I should rightly say, now we know he is the chosen one."

"King Max!" snorted Pa. "I'm never going to get my tongue around that."

"Take it from me, my dear chap," said Uncle B. "Your son is the elected ruler of hedgehogkind – it's as plain as

the snout on your face. What other
hedgehog has ever before worn a
crown that flashes blue light? We are
his subjects, all of us."

At this point Max came through a
hole in the hedge that separated
Numbers 5A and 5B.

"I'm starving," he said. "Any grub
left?"

"No," said Pa shortly.

"Oh sire!" cried Uncle B., blinking at the flashing light. "I should have kept some for you. Please forgive me. Let me see now – can I fetch you some snails? Or would Your Majesty prefer worms? Or beetles?"

"Oh, don't get your prickles in a twist," said Max rudely. "Another time, just make sure you leave me some food."

"Now look here, my boy . . . !" began Pa angrily, but the King of the Hedgehogs had already trotted off.

"Max!" shouted Pa. "Stop, d'you hear me? I want a word with you," and he hurried after his son. Cheeky young devil, he said to himself, talking to B. like that. I'll give him a piece of my mind, king or no king.

Max had already crossed the road and was about to make for the Park gates when he heard Pa's voice. He turned round to see his father step off the pavement without looking to left or right, and at that moment a car came round the next corner. The beam of its headlights fell full upon Pa, who instantly rolled into a ball, right in the middle of the road.

"Pa!" cried Max, and rushed back.

Some humans are kindly and some are cruel, and it so happened that the driver of this particular car was the sort of person for whom squashing hedgehogs was fun.

Slowing down a little – for he wanted to make sure of hitting his target – he steered deliberately to run over Pa.

Just then he saw, out of the corner of his eye, a light, a blue light, a flashing light, coming quickly, very low down,

across the road. It was a light, what's more, that seemed to be fixed to the head of another hedgehog!

At this uncanny sight, he wrenched wildly at his steering-wheel and there was a loud crash as he missed Pa and hit a red pillarbox on the pavement.

As the driver sat, half-stunned, in his wrecked car, Pa unrolled to find his son staring anxiously at him.

"Pa! Pa! Are you all right?" cried Max.

"Of course I'm all right," growled Pa furiously. "And no thanks to you. It's all your fault. I shouldn't have come out if it hadn't been for you and your rudeness, you young whippersnapper. Talking to your Uncle B. like that! Who do you think you are?"

I think I'm the King of the Hedgehogs, thought Max, but perhaps I'd better not say so just at this moment. So he said nothing, and Pa turned and went back under the gate of Number 5A, grumbling loudly to himself.

By the time the police arrived, the driver had got out and was looking dazedly at his car and the pillarbox, both busted.

"What happened?" said one of the two policemen.

"It was a hedgehog," said the driver.

"A hedgehog?"

"Well, two hedgehogs actually."

"Made you swerve, eh?" said the other policeman.

"Yes."

"Overdid it a bit, didn't you?"

"So would you have done," said the driver. "One of them had a light on his head."

"One of the hedgehogs?"

"Yes."

"Had a light on his head?"

"Yes. A blue flashing light," said the driver. "A revolving one." He pointed at the police car. "Just like you've got," he said.

"I see," said the second policeman.

He went to the police car and took out a breathalyser kit.

"Now sir," he said. "I'd like you to blow into this, please."

Chapter 5

THE SCIENTISTS' NOTES of the next night made interesting reading.

10.39 pm. Located E.E. near Park gates. Radio contact excellent and light still working well. It is now apparent that ownership of this flashing light has made E.E. the dominant individual amongst local hedgehog community. Prof D. and Dr D-G. observed a number of animals approaching E.E. in what was obviously a respectful manner, some even curling into a ball before him. E.E. appeared to be searching (for a mate?), but apparently without success.

*11.15 pm. A crowd of hedgehogs
(presumably of both sexes), adults,
juveniles and some very young specimens,
followed closely at E.E.'s heels as he
criss-crossed the Park. Is this close
attention inspired by E.E. as an
individual? Or by his light? Or both?
At all events E.E. reacted against this
show of respectful interest and at 11.35 pm
suddenly turned on his followers, apparently
in anger. All then dispersed, as though in
obedience to an order, leaving E.E. alone.*

47

*11.40 pm. Heavy downpour of rain began,
causing slugs and snails to show much
activity. E.E. feeding greedily.*

*11.53 pm. Prof D. and Dr D-G.
discontinued observation in order to seek
shelter. However, on way out of Park, at
12.00 midnight precisely, Prof D. noticed
pale shape in shrubbery at edge of
Ornamental Gardens. On inspection, this
proved to be an albino hedgehog, the spines
white, the pupils of the eyes pink, a young
healthy specimen. It was decided to test
E.E.'s reaction to this unusual animal,
which was therefore caught (in Dr D-G.'s
hat) and taken back to location of last
sighting of E.E.*

*12.12 am. Albino hedgehog released before
E. E. but showed no signs of respect for
him (weak eyesight?). E.E. however
appeared excited and interested. (Note:
albinism in hedgehogs is unusual rather*

than rare; however neither Prof D. nor
Dr D-G. have ever encountered one, nor,
patently, had E.E.) Much squeaking and
grunting occurred. Without warning,
albino hedgehog attacked E.E., biting his
snout and then making off.
Observation ended 12.14 am.

"Ow! That hurt!" cried Max, but
there was no answer as the pale
stranger hurried away.

Max felt really sorry for himself for a
moment. What a night! he thought.
First I get a rocket from Pa, then I
have to put up with all those hogs
bowing and scraping to me ("Yes,
Your Majesty! No, Your Majesty!
Three bags full, Your Majesty!"), and
then a crowd of them follow me about
the place, spoiling my hunting, until I
lose my temper and tell them to buzz

off ("Oh, ever so sorry, Your Majesty!").

But then I thought things were really taking a turn for the better. Nice drop of rain, a jolly good bellyful of slugs and snails, and finally, to cap it all, this absolutely fantastic girl appears, white as snow, with lovely pink eyes! There's my Queen, I thought, watch me chat her up.

He had moved towards her confidently, his crown of light flashing on her so that her pale spines looked bluish and her eyes glistened redly. What a smasher! thought Max.

"Hi there, baby!" he cried. "What do they call you?"

"My name," said the albino hedgehog in a chilly voice, "is Bianca, and I am not a baby, and my mother brought me up not to speak to strange boars. So why don't you get lost?"

"Hey, hey!" said Max. "You can't talk to me like that. Don't you know who I am?"

"No," said Bianca, "and I don't want to."

"But I'm the King of the Hedgehogs," said Max. "King Max the First, that's me. Can't you see my crown?"

"Yes," said Bianca. "It hurts my eyes. Turn it off."

I can't, thought Max.

"I don't wish to," he said, "and anyway you should address me as Your Majesty. But I'll let you off, seeing what a popsy you are. Come on now, Bianca, let's get together."

"We'll get together all right," said the albino hedgehog, and with that she bit Max sharply on his snout, before hurrying off into the darkness.

But though Professor Duck and Dr Dandy-Green witnessed E.E. being attacked, they could not know what was going on in his mind, even as he nursed his sore and bleeding nose.

Oh Bianca! he was thinking. Oh what a girl! What beauty! And what spirit!

The scientists could not possibly have been aware that Victor Maximilian St George was head over heels in love.

Chapter 6

THE ARRIVAL OF the palely beautiful
Bianca caused havoc among the young
hedgehog boars in the Park and its
surroundings. None had ever seen
anything like her, and all were deeply
attracted.

To Max's great annoyance, many of
them took to following her about.
Suppose she should choose one of them
as her mate? Max couldn't bear the
thought of it.

He summoned Peony, Pansy and
Petunia.

"Pass the word," he said to them.

"All young male hedgehogs to attend a meeting tonight. In the Bandstand. By order of the King."

"All young males?" said Peony.

"Wow!" said Pansy.

"Can we come to the meeting?" said Petunia.

"Certainly not," said Max. "Go on now, off with you."

"OK, Sire," they squeaked, and they ran away, giggling as usual.

By now there wasn't a hedgehog in the area that cared to disobey the King, so that the Bandstand was packed that evening. Once again Max placed himself in the centre of the circular interior, the flashes from his revolving light playing upon the faces of the audience.

No one noticed the two humans, one

holding a receiver, who stood silent in
the darkness outside.

"I have called you here tonight,"
said Max in what he thought was a
regal voice, "to express my displeasure
at the behaviour of some among you
towards a newcomer to our society, a
newcomer, I may say, of a different
colour."

"Bianca!" said someone at the back
softly.

"She has not been treated with

proper respect," said Max, "and I
have no doubt that she is upset by
your unwanted attentions. These
attentions will cease, as of now. Is that
clearly understood?"

"Yes, Your Majesty," said a number
of grudging voices, and Max swept out
of the Bandstand in what he thought
was a regal manner.

9.42 pm. (ran the scientists' notes
next day)
*Large assembly of hedgehogs within
Bandstand. E.E. at centre. Much
grunting from E.E. who then departed. As
soon as he had gone (9.58 pm), remainder
burst out into loud chorus of squeaks,
squeals, snorts and grunts which continued
until 10.02 pm.*

Once Max had left the Bandstand, a
babble of voices arose.

56

"That's it then, boys. We've had it."

"Fancies her himself, the King does."

"She'll make a lovely Queen, mind."

"Bit of all right, isn't she?"

"Talk about crumpet!"

"Those pale spines!"

"Those pink eyes!"

"What a dish!"

"But not for you, mate."

"What's he got that I haven't got?"

"A crown of light, mate, that's what."

"Oh, see if I care. There's plenty of other fish in the sea," one said and went off, shrugging his spines.

Discreetly followed by Professor Duck and Dr Dandy-Green, Max hurried about the Park, looking for Bianca.

I got off on the wrong foot last night,

he said to himself. I was too pushy, and anyway she didn't like all that King business. I must sweet-talk her. Flattery never fails, they say.

When he did at last find the albino sow, she was making her way from the Lily-Pond to the Ornamental Gardens. Max hid himself and his light till she had gone by. It had occurred to him that it would be a good thing to turn up with a present, and at that moment Fortune favoured him.

A slithering sound alerted him, and then he saw the sinuous shape of a small grass-snake, winding its way through a flower border.

Max ran forward.

With one bite he killed it, and then, carrying its still writhing body in his mouth, hurried after the albino.

"Hello, Bianca!" cried Max with his

mouth full, and then, dropping the snake before her, "I've brought you a present."

Bianca turned, her pink eyes blinking in the flashes of blue light.

"Oh, it's you again, is it?" she said. "Looking for another bite on the nose, are you, your flipping majesty?"

"No, no," cried Max hurriedly. "It's just that I simply had to come and tell you how beautiful I think you are. I've never seen a hedgehog like you before."

"Don't suppose you have," said
Bianca. "Thanks for the snake
anyway. And goodbye."

"But I want us to be . . . friends,"
said Max.

"Fat chance," said Bianca.

She took a large bite from the tail of
the snake.

Max took a deep breath.

"Bianca," he said. "Will you marry
me?"

"Not on your nellie," said Bianca.

"But why not? What's wrong with
me?"

Bianca swallowed her mouthful.

"Look, King Max or whatever your
silly name is," she said. "Get this in
your royal nut. For my money, you are
a weirdo."

"Whatever d'you mean?" muttered
the King of the Hedgehogs.

"Well, I ask you!" said Bianca. "Talk about freaks! Just take a look at yourself. With that stupid thing stuck on your head and that absolutely maddening blue light flashing the whole time, you'd drive a girl up the wall, you would. If that's what kings look like, give me a common or garden hedgehog any night."

10.22 pm. Followed E.E. from Bandstand towards Lily-Pond. Albino hedgehog sighted here. E.E. killed grass-snake in flower border in Ornamental Gardens. Carried same and presented to albino (albino possibly female? Courtship behaviour?)
10.31 pm. Leaving albino to eat snake (tail first), E.E. returned to Lily-Pond. At edge of pond did not drink but appeared to be studying own reflection in the water.

62

*After a while, E.E. moved slowly off.
Observation of E.E. discontinued (10.33
pm) in order to return to study albino's
consumption of snake. Head of snake
disappeared 10.42 pm.*

With Bianca's words ringing in his
ears, Max had made his unhappy way
to the Lily-Pond. "Just take a look at
yourself," she had said. He would. He
did.

He stood at the rim of the pond and
looked down at the still surface, seeing
himself and his crown of light for the
first time. Did he not look every inch
the King?

Yet she had called him a weirdo.

What was he to do?

He did not want to give up his royal
position. He liked being King Max the
First.

Yet Bianca had said, "Give me a common or garden hedgehog any night." Bianca, whom he must make his bride or die of a broken heart.

So there was no choice. His crown
must go. He must get rid of it. But
how?

He shook his head violently but the
transmitter was much too firmly fixed,
and no amount of rubbing it against
trees or bashing it against walls shifted
it an inch.

He was stuck with it. And because of it he would lose the love of his life.

At that moment Max who had once thought himself a hodgeheg, Max the pioneer of road safety, Max the hero of hedgehogkind, Max the First, ruler of his people, became simply a most unhappy young hog who badly needed a mother's comfort, and he set off for home. In such a whirl were his thoughts that when he reached the road opposite Number 5A, he simply stepped straight off the pavement without looking.

Chapter 7

IN FACT HE stepped straight into the
path of a large lorry, which braked and
stopped, just in time.

Some humans are kind and some are
cruel, and it so happened that the
driver of this particular lorry was the
sort of person who would not hurt a
fly, much less a hedgehog.

Now he climbed down from his cab
and, blocking Max's further progress
with one large boot, looked in
amazement at what was before him.

"'Ooever done that to you, old
chap?" said the lorry driver softly.

"Kids, I reckon, out of devilment. I've 'eard of 'em tyin' tin cans to cats' tails, that's bad enough but I never seen nothing like this before. A toy light'ouse it looks like, stuck on a poor bloomin' 'edge'og. What a trick to play! Never you mind, old son. I'll soon 'ave that off you."

He picked Max up by his crown, and, climbing back into his cab, got out his tool-box. One tap from a hammer and the flashing light flashed no more. One squeeze from a pair of pliers ensured that the transmitter would never again transmit. Then, very carefully so as not to hurt the tightly curled animal, the lorry driver picked off, bit by bit, the rest of the apparatus so carefully glued on by Professor Duck and Dr Dandy-Green, until at last Max was his old self again.

"There!" said the lorry driver. "That's better."

He climbed down again, holding Max wrapped in a piece of rag, and looked about him. Opposite, he could see, were some suburban gardens and he crossed the road towards them.

"Now then," he said, "you take a bit of advice from me, old feller. Don't go crossin' any more roads, see? There ain't an 'edge'og in the world as ever found a safe way to cross roads." And he pushed Max underneath the nearest garden gate. On it was its number – 5A.

Max remained rolled up in a ball as the lorry drove away, wondering what it was that some human had done to him now. When he uncurled, his eyes told him that the night was dark, just like nights used to be. No blue light

flashed about him. Then his nose told
him where he was. Then his ears heard
the sound of shrill voices.

"Ma! Pa! Our Max has come
home!" squeaked his three sisters.

In a moment Max was surrounded
by his family.

"Oh Max!" Ma cried. "You've lost
your crown!"

"Feels like it," said Max.

"Does that mean I'm no longer the
mother of a king?"

"Looks like it," said Max.

"So we're not princesses?" cried
Peony, Pansy and Petunia.

"Seems like it," said Max. "I'm just
my old self again."

"Good," said Pa.

Uncle B. came hurrying through the
hedge.

"Oh Sire!" he cried. "Whatever has

befallen Your Majesty?"

"I'm not my majesty any more, Uncle B.," Max said. "And by the way, I'm very sorry I was rude to you the other evening."

"Good," said Pa.

"Oh, that's quite all right, Your . . . I mean, Max," said Uncle B.

71

He sounded depressed at this abrupt end to his dreams.

"Cheer up, B.," said Pa. "It looks like that's the first and last time anyone's going to believe in that story about a King of the Hedgehogs."

Uncle B. sighed deeply.

"In fact," chuckled Pa, "you might say that King Max the First is also King Max the Last."

"Never mind, Max dear," said Ma. "You'll always be a king in my eyes."

That's what I came home for, thought Max, to be comforted by my mum.

And why did I need comforting?

Because Bianca didn't like me.

And why didn't she like me?

Because I had all that stuff on my head.

But I haven't got it any more!

"Thanks, Ma," he said. "And now I must be going. I have to meet someone."

"A girl!" cried Peony, Pansy and Petunia with one voice.

"Someone special, Max dear?" asked Ma.

"Yes," said Max. "Very special."

"Thinking of settling down, are you?" asked Pa.

"Yes, Pa," said Max. "If she'll have me."

"Take my tip, son," said Pa. "Always agree with everything she says. That's what I've always done with your mother."

"Oh Pa!" squeaked Ma. "The things you say!"

"I hope you have good fortune, Max," said Uncle B. and as he slipped under the gate, Max could hear them all wishing him well.

"Good luck, Max," they cried. "Good luck!"

Because of her colour, Max found Bianca quite easily. She was on her own in the children's playground in one corner of the Park, hunting for woodlice.

Max did not approach her directly but pottered about as though he too was hunting. He watched her all the while out of the corner of his eye, thinking how lovely she looked.

Gradually he moved nearer until he was within speaking distance. Then, politely, he said, "Good morning."

I suppose she'll say, "Oh, it's you again, is it?" he thought. Or she may give me another bite.

But Bianca looked up and answered, "Good morning!" in what sounded quite a pleased sort of voice.

She doesn't recognize me! thought Max.

"Do you know," said Bianca, "that you're the first boy who's spoken to me for ages? Females have been quite polite to me, and one or two old boars, but you're the first young male to say a word to me. All the rest have just pushed off as soon as they saw me coming. I can't think why."

I can, said Max to himself. King's orders.

"Anyone would think I had bad breath or smelled nasty or something," said Bianca. "I haven't, have I? I don't, do I?"

"No, certainly not," said Max. "Your breath is as sweet as the night breeze and you smell of wildflowers."

At this speech Bianca looked more carefully at him with her poor-sighted pink eyes.

"Your voice is familiar," she said. "Do I know you?"

"My name is Victor Maximilian St George," said Max.

"That's a mouthful," said Bianca. "Do people call you that?"

"No. Just Max."

"Funny," said Bianca. "I met another chap called Max recently. It

must be a common name round these
parts."

"What was he like, this other
chap?" said Max.

"A proper bighead," said Bianca. "Called himself the King of the Hedgehogs, if you please. Wore a thing on his head with a flashing light on it. Talk about a show-off! Fancied himself rotten, he did. I soon saw him off, I can tell you."

Max wrinkled his nose.

"I bet you did," he said. "He sounds awful. I'm not a bit like that. I'm just a common or garden hedgehog."

"Oh, I wouldn't say that," murmured Bianca.

Max gulped.

"What would you say?" he asked.

"I'd say you were quite a nice-looking boy," said the albino sow. "By the way, my name's Bianca."

"Oh," said Max.

"D'you like woodlice?"

"Yes."

"Have one of mine."

"Oh thanks," said Max. "D'you think . . . can . . . could . . . would . . . d'you think we could meet again? Go for a walk perhaps?"

"I don't see why not," said Bianca.

Chapter 8

"I'M AFRAID WE'VE lost him," said
Professor Duck.

"Looks like it," said Dr
Dandy-Green.

The two scientists were sitting in
their laboratory some days later.

For several nights now they had
combed the Park from end to end and
explored all the suburban gardens, but
without success.

"Even if his light had failed," said
Dr Dandy-Green, "the transmitter
should have been working. Yet we've
not picked up any signal at all."

"I fear we must admit," said the professor, "that E.E. is no longer with us. He might just have moved to another territory, I suppose, but I think it much more likely that he has shared the fate of so many hedgehogs."

"Been run over, you mean?" said the doctor.

"Yes."

"Yet he was so careful. You remember that time we saw him crossing a road? Anyone would think he'd learned the Green Cross Code. Extraordinary really, the things we've observed."

"Yes. There was that road crossing, and then all that business of hedgehogs queuing up to be inspected by him."

"And the way they all followed him about the Park."

"And that great crowd that

surrounded him in the Bandstand the
second time, as though he were making
a speech to them."

"We may have lost him," said Dr
Dandy-Green, "but think what we've
gained – enough material for us to
write a revolutionary paper upon the
behaviour of Erinaceus Europaeus. No
one has ever before witnessed such
scenes."

"We shall astonish the scientific
world," said Professor Duck.

"And we mustn't forget to mention the albino," said Dr Dandy-Green. "Quite a rarity among hedgehogs."

The professor sighed.

"Yes," he said. "If indeed it was a sow, I just wish that it could have paired off with our friend E.E. They'd have made a lovely couple."

Even as the two men spoke, Max and Bianca were breakfasting together in the Ornamental Gardens. It had been a wet night, bringing out a mass of slugs and snails as usual, and they squatted side by side, the handsome young boar and the beautiful young sow, their jaws working rhythmically.

After a while Max spoke.

"You know that chap you were telling me about – the one with all that stuff on his head?"

85

"Yes," said Bianca. "Called himself King Max the First, would you believe it?"

King Max the Last, thought the ex-monarch.

"What else did he say to you?" he went on.

"Asked me to marry him!" said
Bianca. "Of all the cheek! And just
supposing I'd fancied him – which I
most certainly did not – just imagine
what our babies would have been like!

Half of them would probably have been born with flashing blue lights on their heads."

Max took a deep breath.

"Our babies wouldn't be like that, Bianca," he said.

Bianca swallowed the snail she was eating and looked directly at him.

"Victor Maximilian St George," she said. "Is that a proposal of marriage?"

"Yes," said Max. "Will you?"

"Yes," said Bianca. "I will."

Also in Young Puffin

THE Hodgeheg

Dick King-Smith

Max is a hedgehog who becomes a hodgeheg, who becomes a hero!

The hedgehog family of Number 5A are a happy bunch, but they dream of reaching the Park. Unfortunately, a very busy ~road lies between them and their goal and no one has found a way to cross it in safety. No one, that is, until the determined young Max decides to solve the problem once and for all...

READ MORE IN PUFFIN

For children of all ages, Puffin represents quality and variety – the very best in publishing today around the world.

For complete information about books available from Puffin – and Penguin – and how to order them, contact us at the appropriate address below. Please note that for copyright reasons the selection of books varies from country to country.

On the worldwide web: www.puffin.co.uk

In the United Kingdom: Please write to *Dept. EP, Penguin Books Ltd, Bath Road, Harmondsworth, West Drayton, Middlesex UB7 ODA*

In the United States: Please write to *Consumer Sales, Penguin USA, P.O. Box 999, Dept. 17109, Bergenfield, New Jersey 07621-0120*. VISA and MasterCard holders call 1-800-253-6476 to order Penguin titles

In Canada: Please write to *Penguin Books Canada Ltd, 10 Alcorn Avenue, Suite 300, Toronto, Ontario M4V 3B2*

In Australia: Please write to *Penguin Books Australia Ltd, P.O. Box 257, Ringwood, Victoria 3134*

In New Zealand: Please write to *Penguin Books (NZ) Ltd, Private Bag 102902, North Shore Mail Centre, Auckland 10*

In India: Please write to *Penguin Books India Pvt Ltd, 706 Eros Apartments, 56 Nehru Place, New Delhi 110 019*

In the Netherlands: Please write to *Penguin Books Netherlands bv, Postbus 3507, NL-1001 AH Amsterdam*

In Germany: Please write to *Penguin Books Deutschland GmbH, Metzlerstrasse 26, 60594 Frankfurt am Main*

In Spain: Please write to *Penguin Books S. A., Bravo Murillo 19, 1° B, 28015 Madrid*

In Italy: Please write to *Penguin Italia s.r.l., Via Felice Casati 20, I-20124 Milano.*

In France: Please write to *Penguin France S. A., 17 rue Lejeune, F-31000 Toulouse*

In Japan: Please write to *Penguin Books Japan, Ishikiribashi Building, 2-5-4, Suido, Bunkyo-ku, Tokyo 112*

In South Africa: Please write to *Longman Penguin Southern Africa (Pty) Ltd, Private Bag X08, Bertsham 2013*